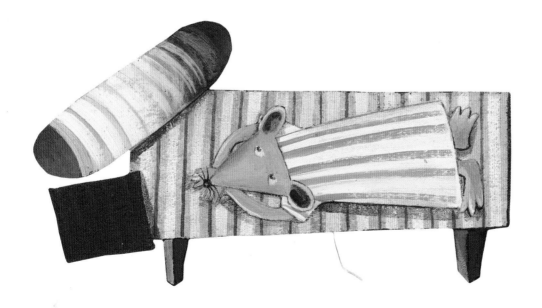

First published © 2015 by Tiny Owl Publishing Ltd
1 Repton House, Charlwood Street, SW1V 2LD, London, UK

Translated by Azita Rassi
Graphic designer: Elahe Javanmard

This edition published in 2017 by Tiny Owl Publishing Ltd

The moral right of Anahita Teymorian as the author and illustrator has been asserted.
Text and illustration ©Anahita Teymorian

ISBN 978-1-910328-21-7

A catalogue record of this book is available from the British Library

www.tinyowl.co.uk
Tiny Owl Publishing Ltd, Registered in England and Wales No. 08297587

The Clever Mouse

Anahita Teymorian

There was once a mouse called Mr Koochi who thought he knew just what he wanted and how to get it.

Mr Koochi Mouse wanted a house, so he set to work, and built himself a little hut home.

"Clever me!" he said.

Next he needed a supply of food, so he set to work and grew wheat, which he ground and made into bread.

"Clever me!" he said. "Now all I need is a wife."

But finding a wife was nothing like building a house, thought Mr Koochi. Then one night he dreamed of what it would be like being married to the Mouse King's daughter, walking together, paw in paw and blissfully happy.

When he woke up next morning, Mr Koochi remembered his dream. "What a good idea," Mr Koochi thought. "Clever me!"

He picked a flower for the princess and set off for the Mouse King's palace.

Mr Koochi knocked at the palace door.

"Who are you, and what do you want?" asked the Mouse King's guards behind the door.

"I have come to ask the princess to marry me," said Mr Koochi.

The guards opened the door. They took Mr Koochi to the Mouse King.

"Why do you want to marry my daughter?" asked the Mouse King.

"Because I dreamed that I was married to her, and it made me happy," said Mr Koochi.

Some of the other mice in the room laughed at that, but the Mouse King held up a paw for silence, and told Mr Koochi, "If you marry my daughter, you won't get any riches. All you'll get is a wife."

"A wife is all that I want," said Mr Koochi. "I already have a home and I grow my own food."

"Good," said the Mouse King. "But will you stay with my daughter no matter what?"

"I will," said Mr Koochi.

"In that case you may go and ask her if she would like to marry you," said the Mouse King.

Princess Mouse's room was in a dark part of the palace. Mr Koochi knocked on her door.

The princess's door opened a little, but all Mr Koochi could see was a bit of a splendid skirt.

He gave a little cough.

"Princess," he said. "My name is Mr Koochi. I am a hard-working and clever mouse who has dreamed of finding happiness with you."

The princess answered, in such a soft kind voice that it made Mr Koochi's heart flutter.

"What do you mean when you use that word 'happiness'?" she asked.

"Happiness," said Mr Koochi, "would be having somebody to love who would love me back. It would mean sharing all the good and the bad things together."

"That's what I want too," said Princess Mouse. "If I agree to become your wife, will you promise never to leave me on my own?"

"I will certainly promise that!" said Mr Koochi.

Princess Mouse got up off her chair and opened the door fully at last.

Now Mr Koochi saw his Princess Mouse bride. She was plump and plain, not at all what he had imagined in his dream or when he had first heard her voice.

"Oh!" he said. "Er ..." He was wondering whether to run away and leave her there, but then he thought how angry that would make the Mouse King and his guards. So Mr Koochi took the Princess Mouse away with him, even though he didn't really want to.

He didn't feel very clever now.

It was a long walk back to Mr Koochi's hut. Princess Mouse wasn't used to walking so far, and it was already getting dark.

"Can we stop and rest for a while?" asked Princess Mouse.

So they sat and ate bread and cheese, which the Princess had carried in her pack, and they decided to stay where they were for the night, and to travel again in the morning.

Princess Mouse fell asleep, but Mr Koochi didn't. He had a mean and cowardly idea. Mr Koochi decided that he could creep away and leave the Princess, and go back to live on his farm by himself. And that's just what he did. He ran away.

When he was far enough away not to be seen, Mr Koochi stopped. I will sleep until morning, he decided, and he undid his pack so that he could use it for a blanket. But his pack wasn't empty. Out of it fell a whole lot of lovely fresh walnuts!

"My favourties!" said Mr Koochi, who hadn't tasted a walnut for a very long time. "What a clever, kind lady the Princess is to have guessed that I love walnuts, and pack them for me!"

As he ate a walnut he felt more and more guilty for having left the Princess after he had promised both her and her father that he would never do that.

"I have been a foolish mouse," said Mr Koochi to himself. "Why should I care whether or not the princess is pretty when she is kind and clever?"

Mr Koochi began to run back to the Princess, hoping to get to her before she woke, but he was too late! He heard the Princess cry out, and when he reached her he found her being robbed by bandits who wanted her crown.

"Leave her alone!" shouted Mr Koochi. He ran at the bandits, pulling them away and hitting them, even though there were too many of them for one mouse to beat.

Then the Mouse King's soldiers came marching along with torches, and the bandits fled. The wise Mouse King had not trusted Mr Koochi to keep his word. Other mice before Mr Koochi had promised to love his daughter, but each of them had run away when they saw that she wasn't beautiful. So the King had sent his soldiers to follow and protect the princess.

"I'm sorry," said Mr Koochi to Princess Mouse. "I am not a clever mouse. I am a foolish and unkind one, and do not deserve a kind and clever lady like you."

"You fought all those bandits on your own, to save me," said the Mouse Princess. "That shows me that we can still find happiness together."

When the Mouse King saw how happy his daughter was with Mr Koochi, and heard the tale of his fighting all those bandits, he smiled.

"You have learned some wisdom from your mistakes," he said. "And you are hard working and you are brave. This mouse kingdom needs a new king. Learn kindness from my daughter, and then I think that you will rule well."

"I am not a clever mouse, but I am a very lucky one!" said Mr Koochi, and he kissed his Princess Mouse bride.

About the book

Mr Koochi is a mouse on a mission. He builds himself a house and grows his own food. 'Clever me!' he thinks. All he needs now is a wife. He decides that a princess wife would suit him very well ... until he finds that the she isn't the princess he dreamt about. Mr Koochi has to learn a hard lesson about kindness to win his princess back.

Anahita Teymorian

Author and illustrator Anahita Teymorian also works with animation in her native Iran. Her books are known all over the world, and her work has been featured in major international exhibitions. She has won awards at the Bologna Children's Book Fair, Noma Concours, and Octagonal in France.
Anahita Teymorian has used a mixed technique for this work, texturing the dark background and scratching out the characters on it.